Ju
296.437
B63   Bogot, Howard.
         Seder with the animals.

Temple Israel Library
Minneapolis, Minn.
———

Please sign your full name on the above
card.

Return books promptly to the Library or
Temple Office.

Fines will be charged for overdue books
or for damage or loss of same.

DEMCO

W9-CHF-762

SEDER WITH THE ANIMALS

By Howard I. Bogot and Mary K. Bogot • Illustrated by Norman Gorbaty

Central Conference of American Rabbis

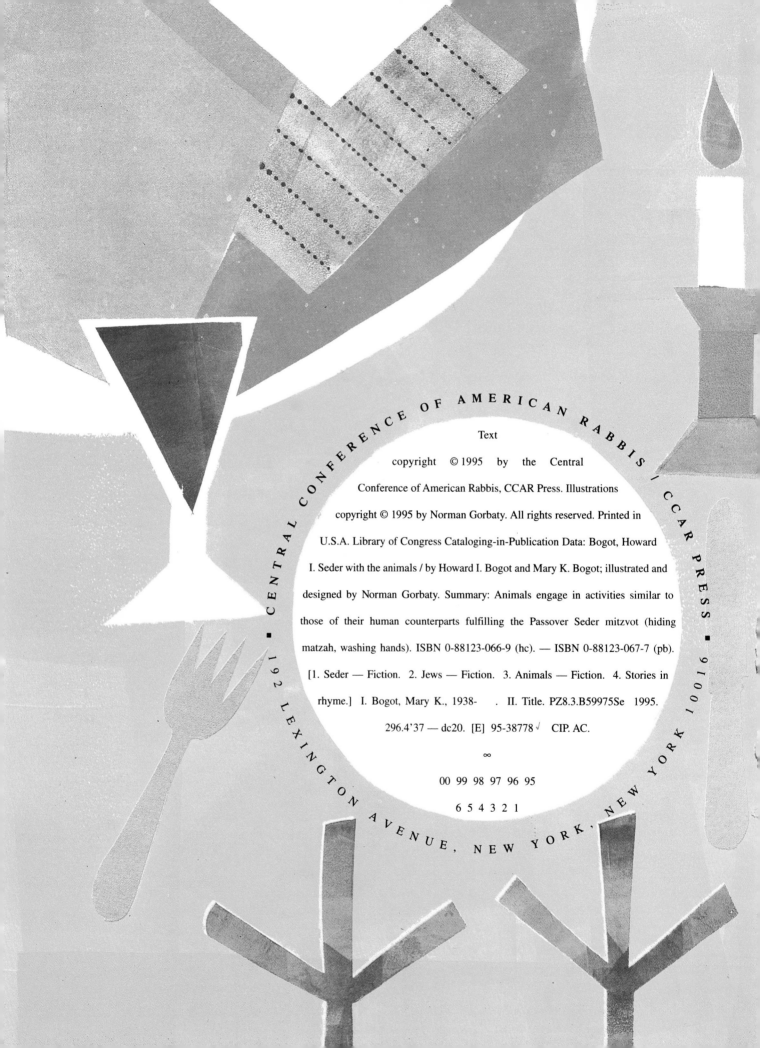

CENTRAL CONFERENCE OF AMERICAN RABBIS / CCAR PRESS ■ 91001 NEW YORK, NEW YORK, NEW YORK AVENUE, 192 LEXINGTON ■

Text copyright © 1995 by the Central Conference of American Rabbis, CCAR Press. Illustrations copyright © 1995 by Norman Gorbaty. All rights reserved. Printed in U.S.A.
Library of Congress Cataloging-in-Publication Data: Bogot, Howard I. Seder with the animals / by Howard I. Bogot and Mary K. Bogot; illustrated and designed by Norman Gorbaty.
Summary: Animals engage in activities similar to those of their human counterparts fulfilling the Passover Seder mitzvot (hiding matzah, washing hands).
ISBN 0-88123-066-9 (hc). — ISBN 0-88123-067-7 (pb). [1. Seder — Fiction. 2. Jews — Fiction. 3. Animals — Fiction. 4. Stories in rhyme.] I. Bogot, Mary K., 1938- . II. Title. PZ8.3.B59975Se 1995. 296.4'37 — dc20. [E] 95-38778 √ CIP. AC.

∞

00 99 98 97 96 95

6 5 4 3 2 1

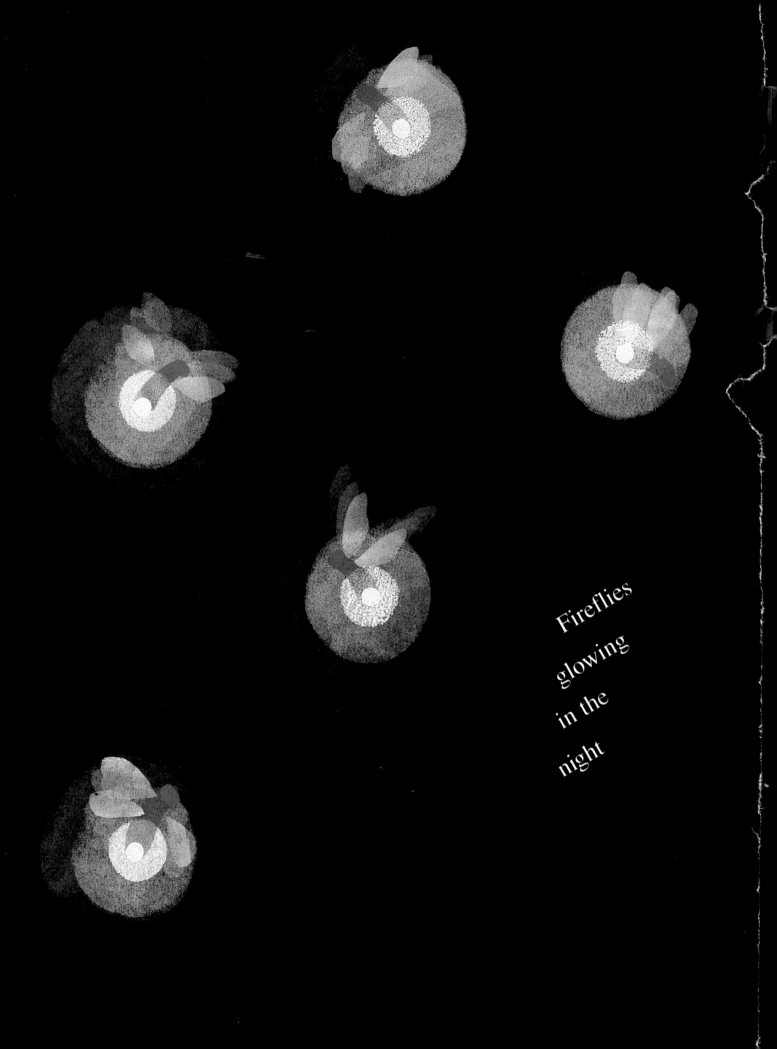

Fireflies
glowing
in the
night

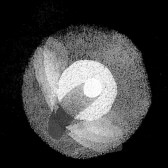

Seder candles   we will light.

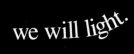

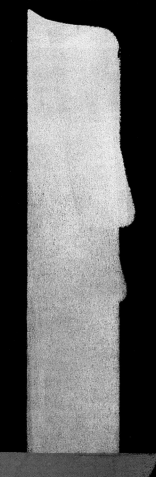
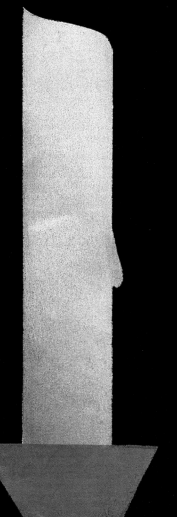

Stomp, stomp, stomp   go elephant feet

Four cups of juice make Pesach sweet.

Spouting whales an ocean scene

Wash seder hands,
wash hands clean.

Caterpillars

chomping

plants

in

spring

Dip greens

in salt

and blessings sing.

Head-in-the-Sand, an ostrich name

Hiding matzah our seder game.

The wise owl

hoots,

then hoots

some more

Seder questions —

one

two

three

four.

Raccoons rinsing paws

By the side of a stream

Wash hands again,

see

how

they

gleam.

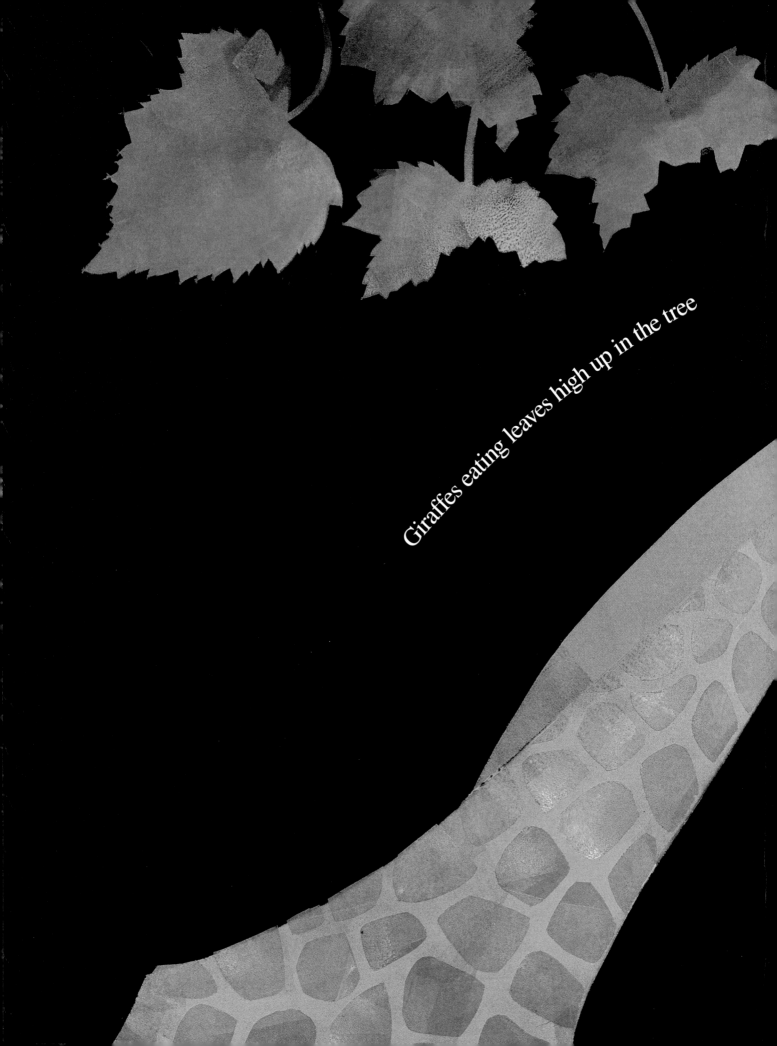

Giraffes eating leaves high up in the tree

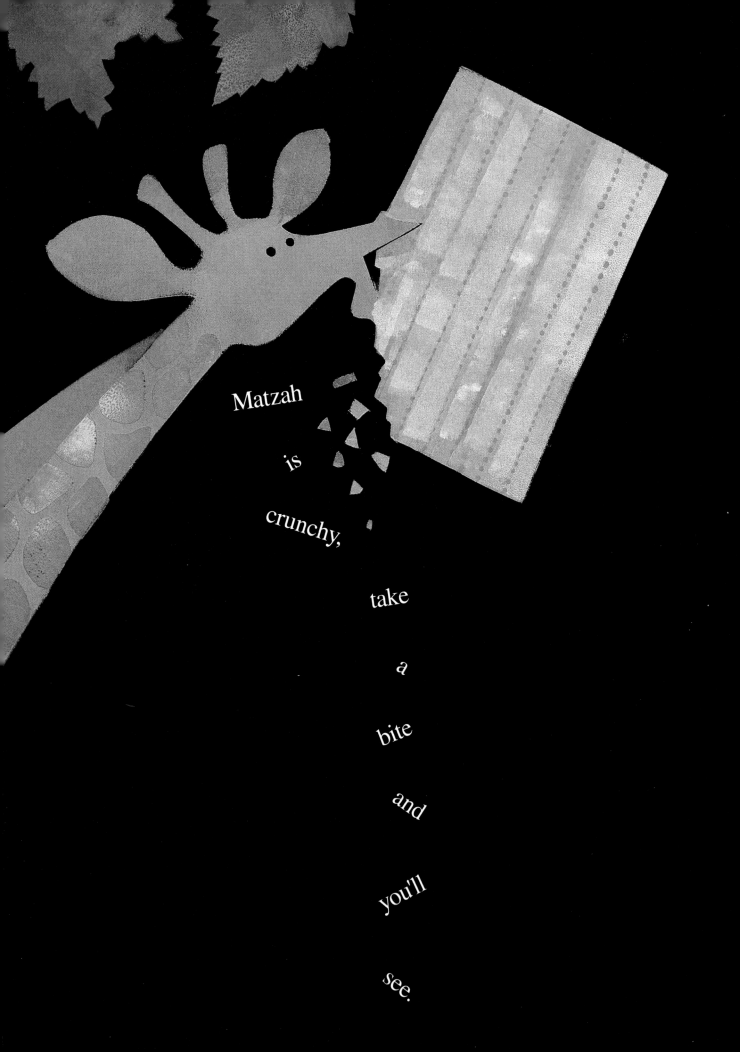

Matzah

is

crunchy,

take

a

bite

and

you'll

see.

Horses gallop,

horses neigh

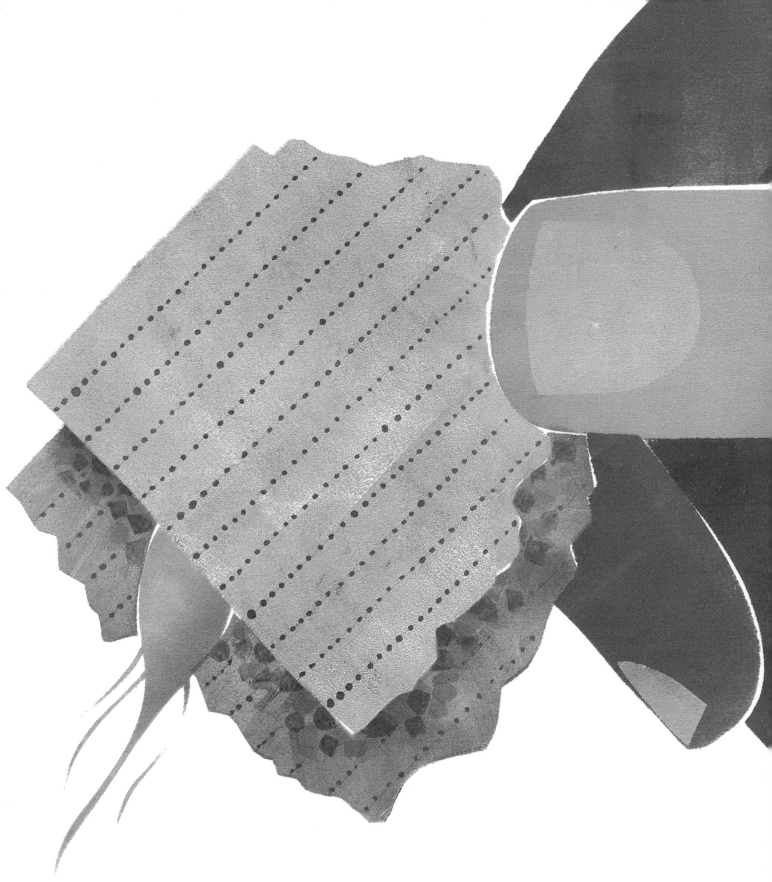

Taste horseradish the Pesach way.

Beavers build homes with mud and twigs

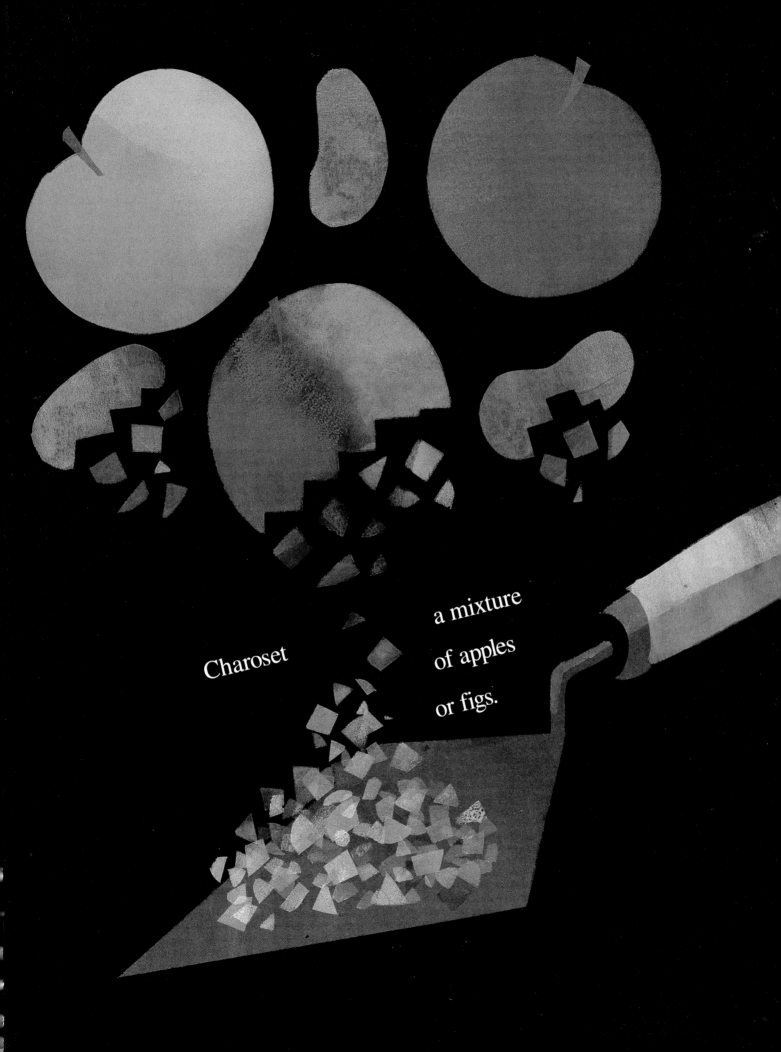

Charoset a mixture of apples or figs.

Sweet honey from the buzzing bee

Dinner served for you and me.

Nuts in winter, a treat for the squirrels

Matzah found by boys and girls.

Animal babies love to play

We sing halleluyah this seder night.

Jerusalem at peace, a world without fear

God bless our seder and the coming year.